I0692191

Color this page

The Colors of Day

Miss Tweedy

Dedicated
to my
grandchildren.

ISBN: 978-1-943960-07-1

Other Titles in this series.

The Colors of Night
The Colors of Spring
The Colors of Summer
The Colors of Fall
The Colors of Winter

Other Picture Books
by this author.

The Shape of Pets
The Shape of Bugs
The Shape of Animals
The Shape of Food
The Shape of Travel
The Shape of Toys

All titles are available in
English, **Spanish** and **French.**

I am
blue;

the

color

of the

sky.

I am
yellow;

the

color

of the **sun**.

I am

brown;

the **color** of the

ground.

I am

green;

the **color** of a **tree.**

I am

purple;

I am

red;

the **color**

of a

bike.

The **colors** of **day**.

red

purple

Try our interactive shape books.

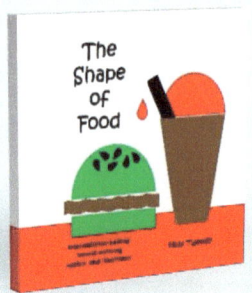
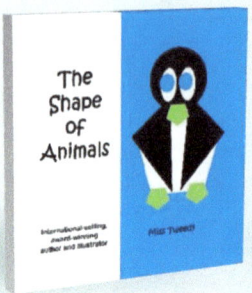

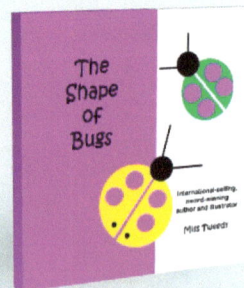

Available in **English, Spanish** and **French.**

Dear Teachers and Parents,

Thank you for purchasing this activity book, with coloring pages and more.

The next two pages contain the wordless story available in the eBook version.

Cut out the strips. Stack them chronologically with number one on top. Align the left edge and staple to create a flip book for your children.

Have
Fun!

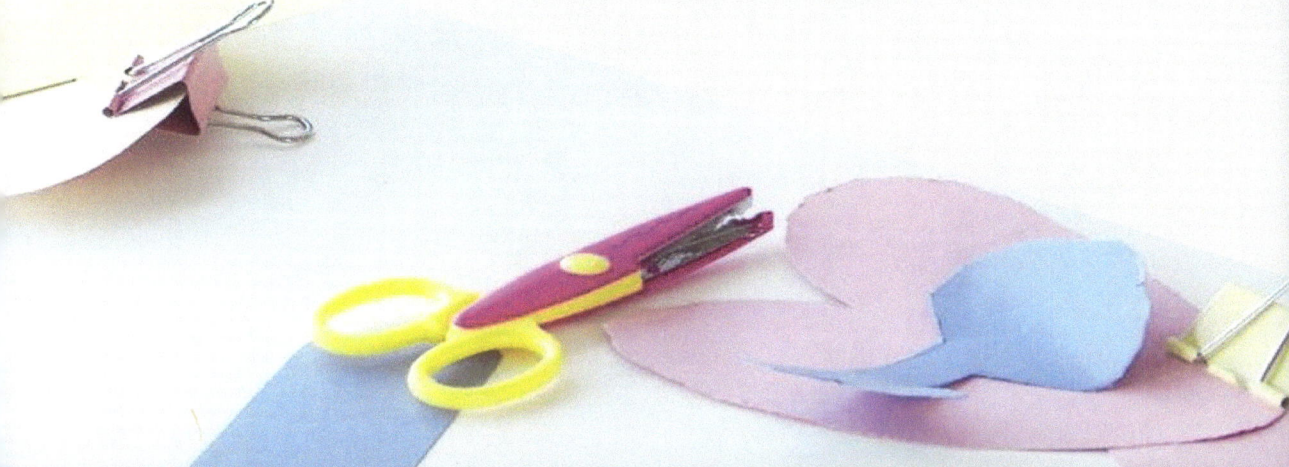

6

5

4

3

2

1

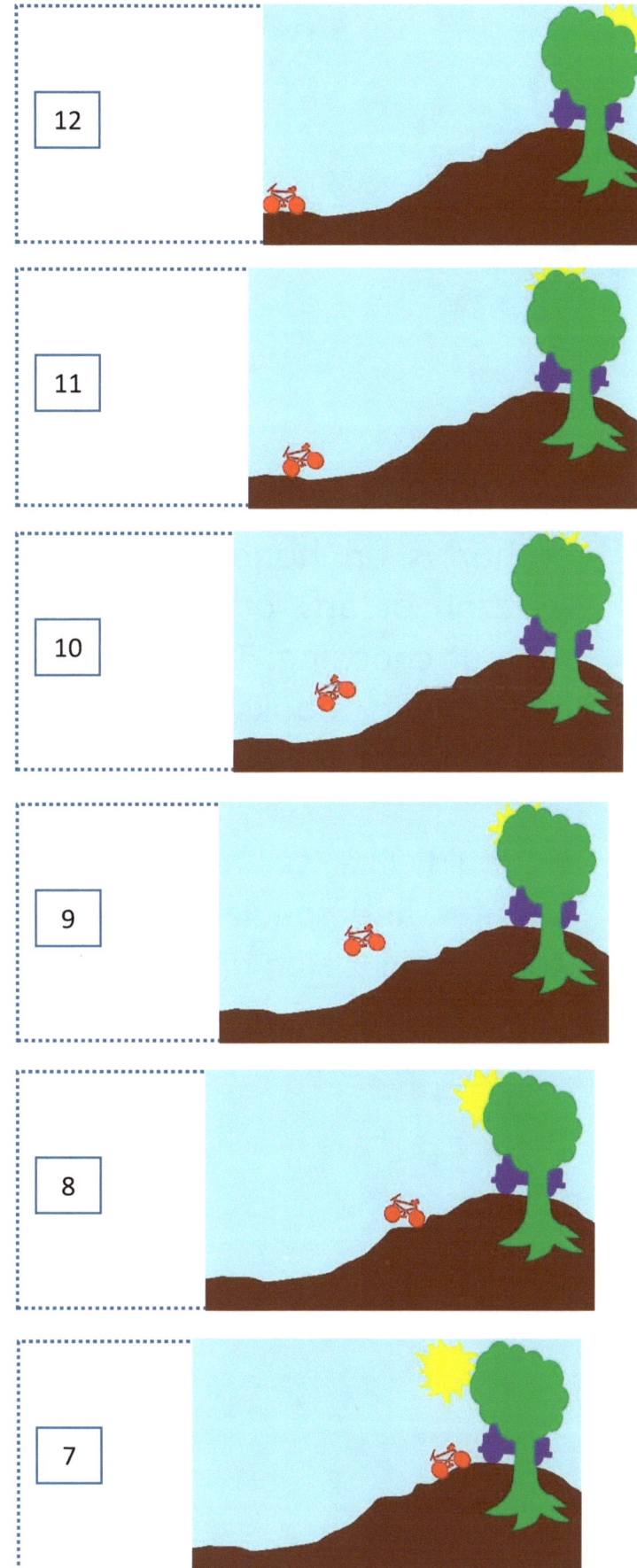

The greatest gift you can give an author is an honest review on Amazon or any other book site of your choosing. This truly does help quality books make it into the hands of other readers.

If you'd like to receive email updates and special offers from Kodzo Books, sign up at:

www.KodzoBooks.com

blue blue

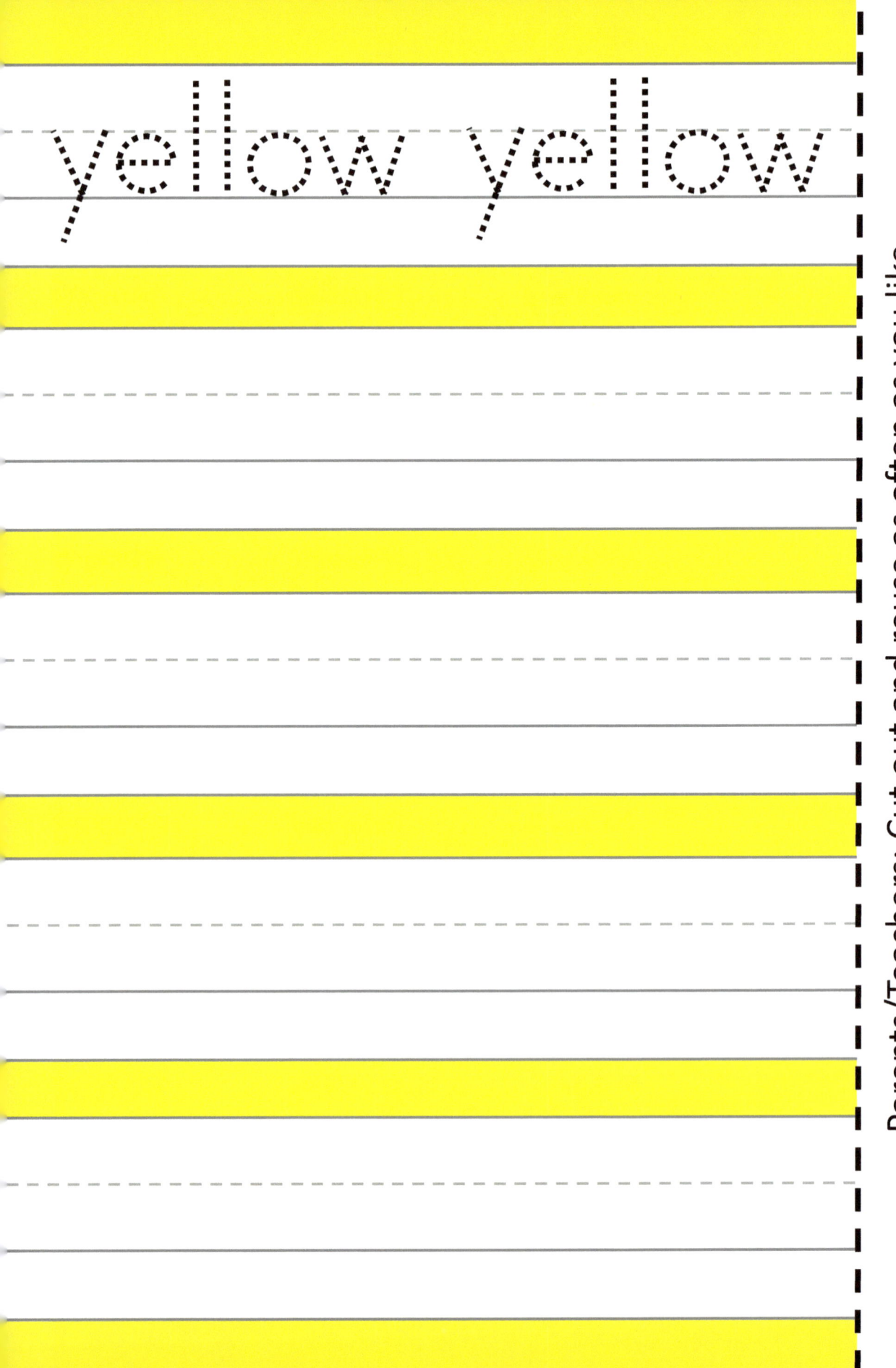

yellow yellow

purple   purple

green green

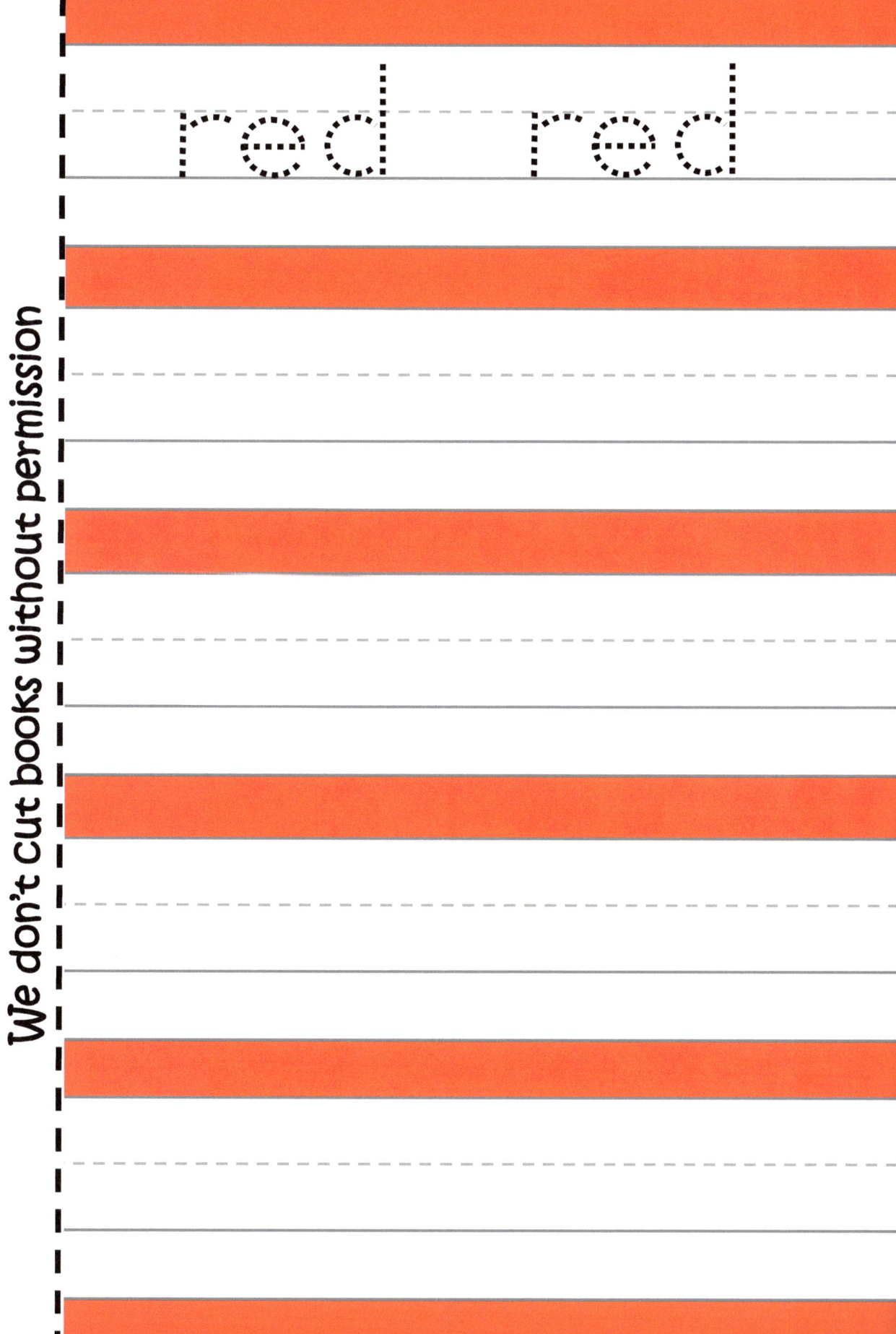

red red

brown brown

Draw a line from the color box to the word

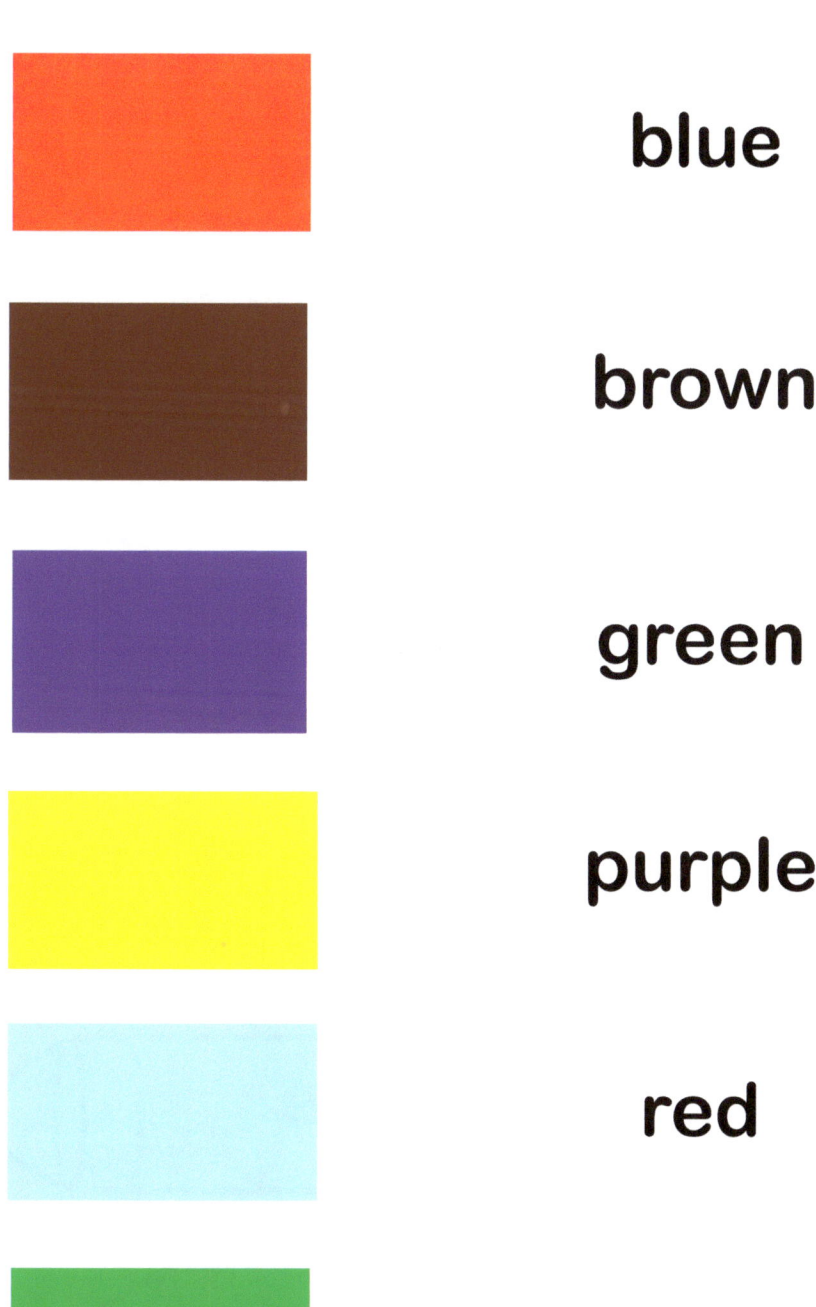

blue

brown

green

purple

red

yellow

Match the colored crayons to the pictures.

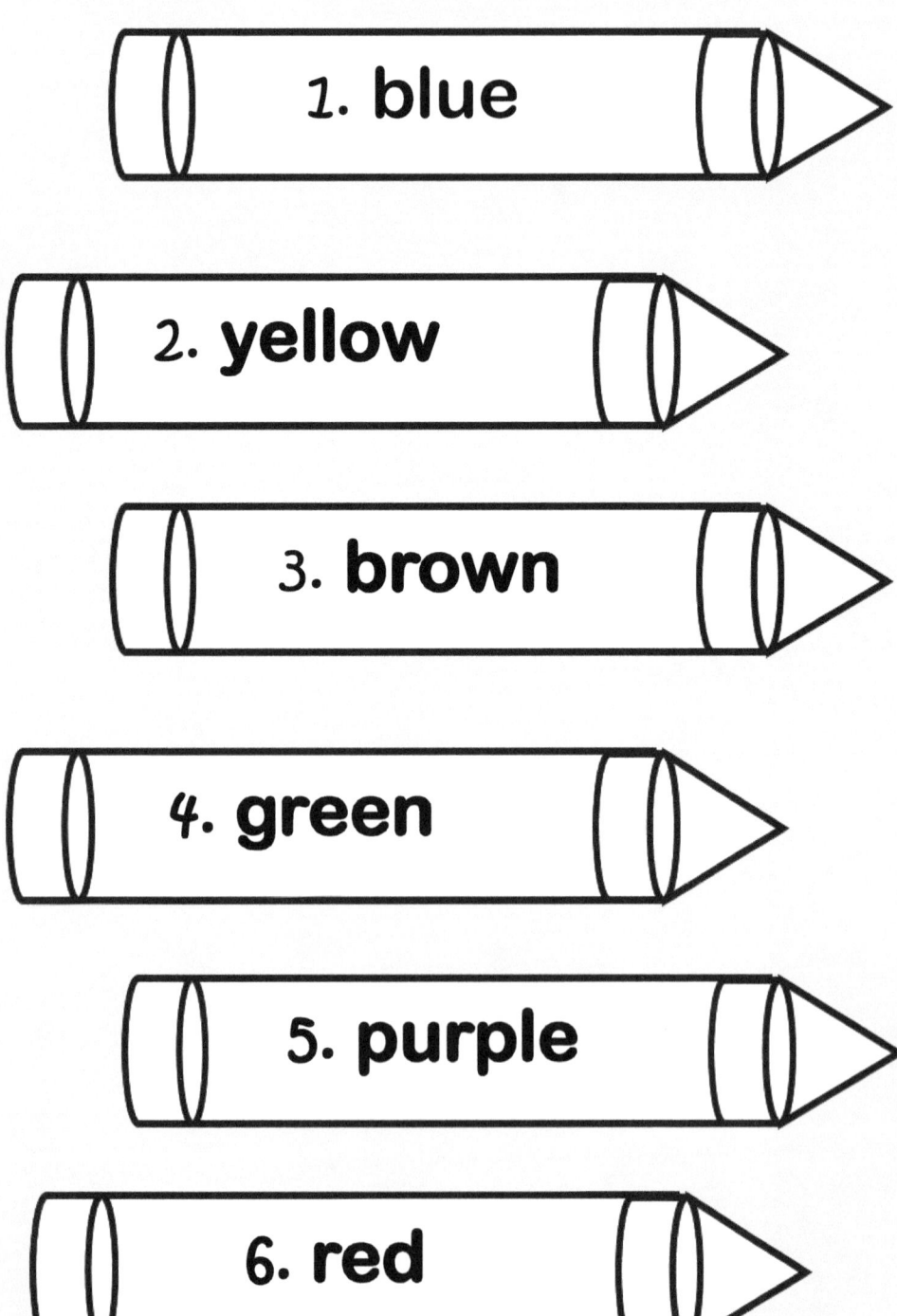

1. blue

2. yellow

3. brown

4. green

5. purple

6. red

Draw a line from the word to right color picture

green

purple

red

yellow

Green

Red

Purple

Parents/Teachers: Cut out and reuse as often as you like.

Brown

Yellow

Blue

Parents/Teachers: Cut out and reuse as often as you like.

24 25 27 28
23 29
22 26
21
20 30 31 32
19 34
18 33 35
17 36
16 37
15 38
14 39
13 12 40
11 41
10 42
9 8 43
7 45
6 5 44
47 46

48

4 49

50
3
61 52
2 55 51
1 54 53
62 60 56
59 57
58

Draw your favorite people into the story.

We don't cut books without permission

Pick any colors to fill in image.

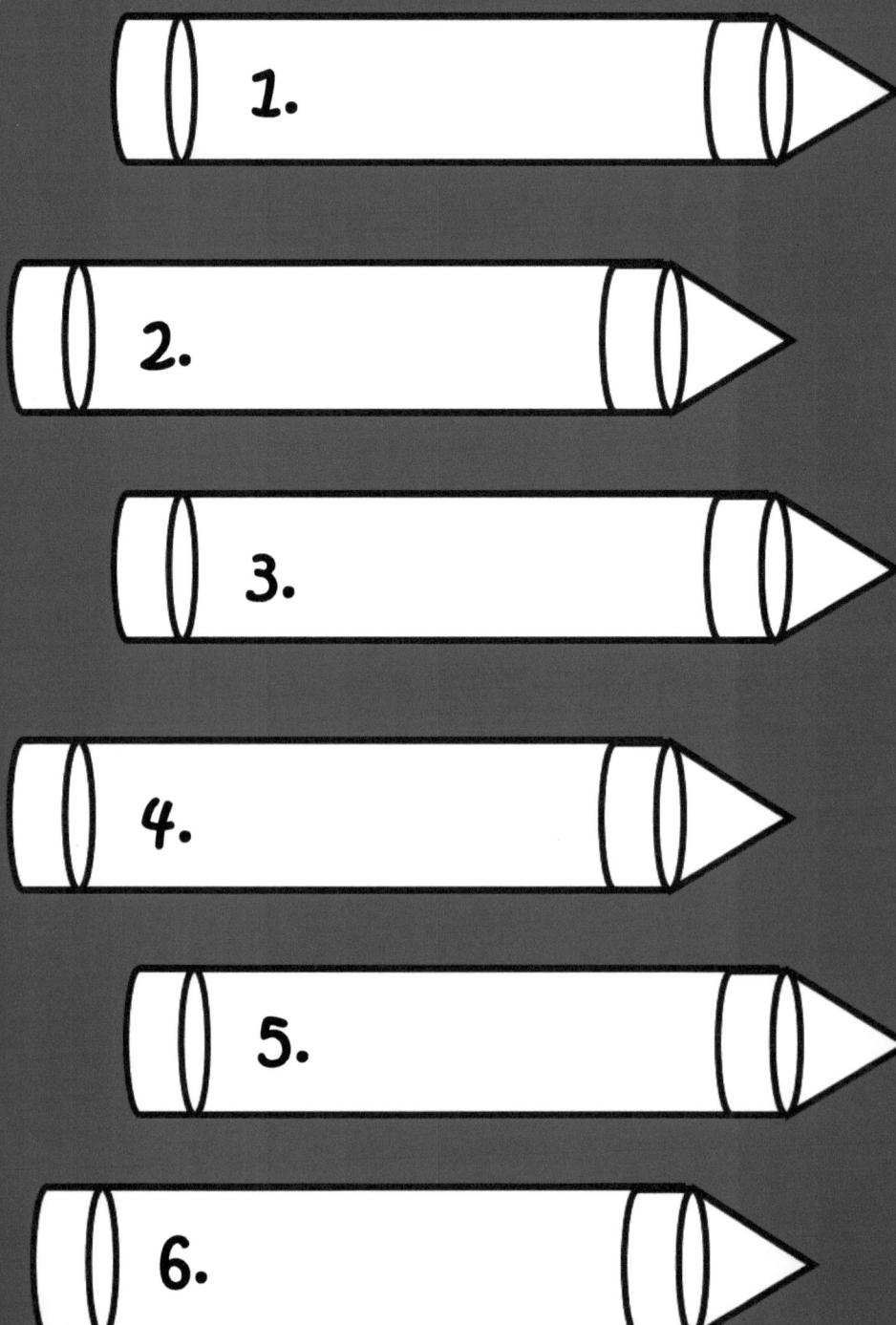

1.

2.

3.

4.

5.

6.

Parents/Teachers: Cut out and reuse as often as you like.

Color this page!

Buy the whole series!